Tally Ho
Palm Beach

by Paul Striberry

ALSO BY PAUL STRIBERRY

Conscious Riding
A Horseman's Diary

Available on Amazon and Kindle

Printed in the United States of America
10 9 8 7 6 5 4 3 2 1

DEDICATION

Thanks to Mary Ann Rogers for the Joyful Hounds, Martin Blunt for the Lobster Quadrille, Teresa Bruni for the layout and design, and Tom Scheve of Orange Publishing.

And Special thanks to Alice
(thanks, Mom).

Table of Contents

*And what is the use of a book,
thought Alice, without pictures or
conversations?*

V

TALLY - OH

A vintage convertible Mercedes hums along Southern Boulevard. The foxy red-head at the wheel is listening to South Florida's AccuWeather forecast. *Palm Beach County is enjoying sunny skies and temperatures in the 80s, while the Northeast is besieged by a January blizzard with gale force winds.*

A white rabbit scurries across the shimmering asphalt and flees into the wilds of Loxahatchee followed by forty foxhounds in full cry. Alice sends the brake to the floorboards, the wheels lock up, the car fishtails, and just misses the pack.

There's a collision of old German steel and creosoted hardwood as the revolving vehicle crashes sidelong into a pile of railroad ties. The doors and fenders are demolished, but for all that, our driver is unhurt.

Staccato notes of a hunting horn fill the air and the earth trembles as a dozen foxhunters gallop out of the orange grove. Horatio J. Hoopes, the maniacal Master of Foxhounds, leads the onslaught. He is well past his prime, clad in scarlet and spurring the flanks of his lathered horse.

"Out of my way!" The Master is livid at the sight of a vehicle merged with his next jump.

Alice endeavors to raise the convertible top but there's only time to duck under the dashboard.

"Tally-Ho" yells Horatio. His brave horse picks up speed in a valiant effort to jump the wreckage, but the sandy soil gives way under Clyde's last stride and cuts down his trajectory. He clears the ties but catches a leg on the car's windshield and flips end over end in a colossal somersault. The Master is catapulted into the air and swan dives onto the pavement.

"Oh no..." Alice peeks out over a crumpled door as another red coated rider gallops toward her.

"Hold Hard." Reginald Ramser reins in just shy of the accident. He is all backbone, most of which has fused over the last six decades. The rest of the riders halt their horses to Alice's unmitigated relief.

"What in blazes?" Ramser's grey beard and military mustache are trimmed to a T, "Who…are…you?"

"Alice Pleasance Liddell," she replies, climbing out of the car and carefully picking her way through the broken glass.

Reginald looks down disdainfully at Alice. "We've lost the hounds and you've spoiled the run. Watch the hunt if you must, but next time don't park behind a jump."

"Park? Are you mad? Your leader is out on the street, this car is demolished and I might have been killed."

"Quite."

"Your dogs ran out and I…"

"They are not dogs, young lady. They are called hounds."

"Then your hounds were running amuck in traffic."

"I hope you didn't hit them." Ramser glances toward the road, ignoring the Master's spread-eagled body.

A police car screeches to a stop and the ambulance arrives minutes later. Two paramedics haul out a defibrillator in a last-ditch effort to save Horatio. A benevolent smile has replaced the rage on the Master's face, however the attendants fail to find his heartbeat so they pack up and haul him away.

"I'll attend to this. Sheriff Coolidge is a friend of mine." Ramser rides over to the patrol car leaving Alice to face the others on her own.

Clayton Hoopes, a lone friendly face in the gathering, removes his top hat and dismounts, "At your service ma'am, is there anything I can do?"

Alice envisions her Phoenix rising from the flames.

"Looks like The Master has jumped his last fence." Clayton smiles quizzically and offers a silver flask.

She takes a sip and shudders.

"It's Courvoisier, the brandy of Napoleon."

"I'm so sorry…"

He tries to put her mind at rest, "Not to worry, death is absolutely safe."

Curiouser and curiouser, Alice thinks to herself.

"I saw the whole thing from the grove. Daddy was a Scorpio, his horoscope said to exercise caution when travelling today."

She tries to smile.

Clayton raises the flask, "To the memory of our illustrious leader chasing Reynard through the Pearly Gates and across the Elysian Fields."

Bruno Mangus rides up leading Horatio's horse. The surly Huntsman's cap and coat are tattered and there's dread in his voice. "The Seminoles got their revenge. The Medicine Man's curse killed him."

"Curse?" Alice's eyes widen.

"That's just superstition," Clayton declares.

Bruno is adamant. "Superstition nothing, the Master dug up Saturiba's grave and killed that red-devil fox with the chief's own tomahawk."

"That was twenty years ago."

"Stone Bear said it would end like this. It's the way of the curse."

Clayton is growing impatient, "Have you collected the hounds?"

"Aye, the brutes were chasing a rabbit." He swings a hunt whip in a menacing arc at the lead hound, but the lash tangles in his horse's tail and Gryphon goes to bucking. The Huntsman loses his seat and wraps his arms around the horse's neck while every fiber in his old red coat stretches to accommodate his bulk.

"Steady now." Clayton catches Clyde's reins and tries to ignore the debacle.

Bruno blows a long sonorous note on his horn, "Come away, come, come, come away," and leads the hounds off toward the kennel.

Victoria Valentine presents herself riding sidesaddle on a dapple grey gelding. "Well, my boy we've certainly had a morning, haven't we?" She is exquisitely attired and a force to be reckoned with.

"I'd like you to meet Alice…" Clayton attempts an introduction.

"Those naughty hounds… Why don't you bring your little vixen to my tea?" Victoria's horse kicks at a horsefly. She taps him with her whip and trots off to a waiting van.

Clayton seconds the motion, "Please come, if you don't have other plans."

Alice looks at the wreck. "Plans…? That Mercedes belongs to the boss, it costs six times my annual salary."

"We'll have it towed to the garage."

They load the horses on a rusting stock trailer and Clayton's old Country Squire chugs off toward Palm Beach.

"I'm so sorry…" Alice is still in shock.

"You did Daddy a favor. The man had a monumental death wish. He was still breaking horses at seventy-five and hunting alligators with a harpoon."

"I'd be happier if a gator cashed his ticket."

"The Master always said, *danger is delectable and risk makes life worth living.* You just spared an old fox hunter his decline."

PALM BEACH

A drawbridge is raised over the Intracoastal Waterway. Clayton is distracted by the restless horses stamping in the trailer.

Alice watches the *SeaScape* sailing southward on a leisurely breeze.

The bridge is lowered and they continue across. At the Bath and Tennis Club, Clayton points his hand out the window for a left turn and cuts off a laundry truck. The angry driver blows his horn.

Alice looks both ways, "No turn signals?"

"The Master never got them fixed. He liked driving the old-fashioned way."

They head down South Ocean Boulevard past Mar-a-Lago's red tile roofs baking in the midday sun.

"Marjorie Post left her estate to the government, but the upkeep was exorbitant so the Feds returned it. Now it's Trumped."

Alice is clearly enchanted by the lofty towers and stately stucco walls. "Have you been inside?"

"In the old days, but the invitations stopped when mother left."

Victoria's seaside manor is a three-story Whitman's Sampler, anchored in a yellow brick courtyard. Clayton zips through the gilded gates and parks the trailer behind a monumental white marble whale encircled by red roses and tiger lilies.

"Horses are banned in Palm Beach, but Moby Dick will hide them from the cops."

The ballroom is a cross between Palm Beach days and Paris nights. Large French windows look out over the Atlantic, but the indigo ocean clashes with the red flocked hearts on the black silk wallpaper.

Victoria emerges from the party, "So glad you've come to enjoy the sun. It's special over here by the sea. I hate to see it set on the wrong side of the lagoon."

Oh? Alice wonders which side is which.

"And where do you live, dear?"

"Over in West Palm, Lake Worth Gardens…"

"Those enormous white condos that look like old cruise ships?"

"The very same…"

"Sorry about your nice car."

"Oh, it's not…" Alice starts to explain, but thinks better of it.

"It's that wretched Seminole curse."

Morals, the inebriated butler arrives with a tray of champagne tipped at a precipitous angle. Clayton rescues two glasses for the ladies. Victoria glides off to greet other guests and the butler imbibes the remaining flute.

Clayton explains, "Morals is the last genuine butler on the island. His great grandfather arrived with the coconuts and planted the first palm trees."

A small round gentleman wearing a red blazer and black gaiters walks gingerly across the room taking three steps forward and one step back.

"Who's that?"

"Eames is the chauffeur."

"Does he drink too?"

"Not a drop. Too many concussions. He's a Great Brit. Came over with the Rolls, drives it on the wrong side… well it's the right side in England, but over here he gets hit head on."

"How did all this money happen?"

"Victoria's third husband was Sutton Van Cleef—Texas oil. He bought her a cow pony and she took him for a ride."

"Where's Sutton now?"

"Back in Houston. When Victoria got tired of him, she hired a Beverly Hills lawyer. Her settlement is recorded in the Guinness Book of Records."

They retreat to a corner and relax on the royal blue settee. Henri, the French chef serves them a cup of mock turtle soup and some heart shaped raspberry tarts.

Alice looks through a scrapbook on the coffee table. There are clippings featuring Victoria's lavish jewelry and generous cleavage. One caption reads, *Victoria Valentine and Clayton Hoopes ringing in the New Year, dancing till dawn at the Looking Glass Ball.*

"Lots of balls," Alice is miffed.

"Victoria says I'm the only one she can waltz with."

"She could probably dance with a broom," Alice remarks grudgingly.

Morals tops up their glasses.

"I should take the horses back." Clayton sets his drink down and heads for the door. "Would you like to see Everglades Hall?"

Alice rises to thank her hostess. "Thanks ever so much for having me, it was lovely."

"Just a simple tea party. You must come again."

"Oh, it's a very grand tea party, a very grand house, and very... Thank you."

The Champagne and the Mock Turtle soup are taking their toll. Alice wanders down a long gallery in search of a powder room. She comes face-to-face with a mirror over the mantle and begins feeling giddy. Certainly, this mirror is melting away like a bright silvery mist.

A portal opens and in a moment, Alice is Through the Looking-glass.

DÉJÀ VU

*T'is Brillig and all mimsy are the orange
groves.*

O nce again, Alice is driving the
boss's Mercedes west on Southern Boulevard enjoying the
golden sunshine and balmy breeze when
out of the blue a White Rabbit in a yellow
waistcoat and tattersall jacket appears in
the road.

It flashed across her mind that *she has never before seen a Rabbit in a Waistcoat.*

But, there is no time to contemplate,
with the hounds following in full cry.

Mozart's Horn Concerto fills the air accompanied by a resounding galumphing.

Alice hits the brakes. The Mercedes spins out skidding in circles. Round and round and round she goes, wondering, *where will the whirling come to an end?* There's a horrendous crash as the car collides with a pyramid of railroad ties and the revolving stops. The doors are crushed and the fenders demolished but as happenstance would have it, our heroine is unharmed.

Horatio rides his horse flat out

Long time the manxome fox he sought

With hounds carefree, so raced on he

Without a doubt or thought

Beware the Jabberwock Alas!

The jaws that bite the claws the catch!

Beware the Caterpillar too

And shun the frumious Bandersnatch

The Jabberwock is vexed by the mangled Mercedes merged with his next jump.

The Master then, with eyes of flame,

Galloped whiffling through the orange groves,

Burbling as he came,

O frabjous day

Tally Ho

Tally Ho — Tally Hay

Get out of my way

He fails to look before he leaps, he gyres and gimbles in the wabe,

On the windshield, he overturns and plummets posthaste to the pave.

Reginald Ramser rides up. He is puffed up and put off. The Red Coated Pillar and Alice stare at each other for some time in silence. At last he addresses her in a languid voice, "Who…are…you, and what are you doing here?"

This is not an encouraging opening for a conversation, but Alice politely tries to explain, "Well, these dogs were chasing a rabbit across the road…"

"First, they are Foxhounds, not dogs. Secondly, it is the Beagles who hunt rabbits."

"Be that as it may, I was enjoying the sunshine when a rabbit and your hounds ran out in front of the car. I braked and we skidded round and round…"

"Well, this was not a convenient place to stop."

There in an oafish mood he stands

The Haughty Hunting Pillar stares

Giving Alice reprimands

And denying hounds are hunting hares.

One two! one two! and through and through

His vorpal tongue goes snicker-snack.

Alice surmises, from all that's said

This hunter's mind is out of whack.

"Is that all you have to say?" Alice asks, swallowing her anger as well as she can and relieved when Ramser rides away to talk to the sheriff.

When the Jabberwock Master leaves with a flare,

From the flames, comes forth his heir.

According to legend, the New Phoenix embalms the ashes of the Old Phoenix and brings them to Heliopolis, the City of the Sun.

After crashing the car, watching the Jabberwock implode, and getting reprimanded by Ramser, Alice is apprehensive.

However, the Hatter is smiling quizzically, (though at the moment, there's little to smile about). He is charming and perplexing, and offers her a libation. *DRINK ME* is beautifully engraved on his silver flask.

She ventures a taste and finds *the brandy is dandy. It has, in fact, a sort of mixed flavor of cherry tart, custard, pineapple, roast turkey, toffee, and hot buttered toast,* and so she finishes it off.

Hatter Waxes Rhetorically

I cathect on a field of light

And only perceive a world that's bright.

We're not our body, we're not our thought

And certainly not all the toys we bought.

We have to admit, in all fairness

What we are is pure awareness

I'll not believe in sadness

I won't believe in grief

I don't even, believe in belief

I enjoy a simple perspective

Optimism is my directive.

Alice thinks to herself,

Some of this sounds a bit berserk

Sorting it out, will be hard work.

BANDERSNATCH

Loyal is the pack through and through

Hunting is what hounds are bred to do

Their leader Bayard and forty first cousins,

Hunt the coyotes and fox by the dozens.

However today they are chasing a rabbit,

Hunting bunnies is not a good habit.

When Bruno strikes his horse,
instead of a hound,

He finds himself en route to the ground.

Alice's instincts tell her to avoid the frumious Bandersnatch who is by turns ominous and obsequious.

APRÈS TEA

After the hunt there's a Long Island Ice Tea party, (tequila, vodka, rum, gin, triple sec, and a splash of cola for the amber tint). Queen Victoria, Mistress of all she surveys, is hosting the gathering, to which she invites the Hatter to invite Alice.

Paul Striberry

Foxhunters live in a Wander-land and Alice is a wanderer at heart.

And so, they arrive at the castle by the sea

Just in time for tarts and tea

Morals the Butler is Tweedle Dum and Eames the Chauffeur is Tweedle Dee.

Says Tweedle-Dum to Tweedle-Dee,

The Queen Victoria is calling me

To talk of several things.

A missing case of fine champagne and tarts that sprouted wings.

The Queen of Hearts

She bought the tarts,

All on a winter's day;

But Tweedle-dum the Butler, ate them straight away.

The Queen of Hearts

Called for more tarts,

And berated the Butler full sore,

So Tweedle-dum baked extra treats,

And vowed he'd drink no more.

"Ditto" says Tweedle-Dee.

"Ditto, ditto!" cries Tweedle-Dum.

Dum's loud *Ditto* repels Alice back through the looking glass and she leaves to join Clayton.

EN ROUTE

The station wagon wends its way through an ungentrified neighborhood of West Palm.

At the Regal Castle Trailer Park,

The Residents Wrestle Flamingoes and Whack Hedgehogs

In a Rousing Round of Croquet

Next Door, at the Tanqueray Funeral Home,

The Undertakers are Painting the Floral Wreaths Red

"It all feels like a dream," says Alice.

"Life is a finite dream in the midst of an infinite mystery. That's what makes it fun," the Hatter replies.

He drives by the First Florida Savings and Loan, "That's our bank."

"Do you-all own it?"

"No, I think they own us."

"They do?"

"Eventually everyone gives up everything." Now he finds the conversation distressing and quickly changes the subject. "Do you hunt?"

"Come Monday, I'll be hunting for a new job."

"I mean foxhunting."

"No, never tried it. What's the point?"

"It's a sport."

"Baseball is a sport."

"How do you figure baseball's a sport and hunting isn't?"

"Two teams play ball of their own volition."

"We have a fox and the hounds."

"I suppose the fox thinks it's sporting to be shredded by a pack of hounds while the fans race around yelling Tally-Ho."

"I don't know, do turkeys enjoy Thanksgiving?"

"Thanksgiving's not a sport either, it's a holiday."

"Then think of hunting as a holiday. The fox routinely gets away. A turkey inevitably ends up in the oven."

Heading west, the waffle brown clouds yield to bright sunshine. On a Loxahatchee sand road, Clayton swerves to avoid a box turtle, "I hate killing things."

"Then, why hunt?"

"Just because, I always have." He wistfully watches as a flock of egrets land amid a herd of Black Angus.

EVERGLADES HALL

A dented mailbox leans on its post having lost its daily joust with the mailman. Clayton gazes at the melancholy brick-pile as if for the first time. "There's no place like home." He slows down on the rutted driveway to spare the horses and then lets them wander off.

Alice surveys broken-down fences and the hordes of dandelions swarming over the neglected lawns. "Must have been lovely."

"Was once. It's all the gardener's fault. He quit right after mother left."

The front door stands ajar, sunbeams glimmer through the cracked window panes illuminating clouds of cosmic dust swirling in the humid air. Well-worn oriental rugs and faded tapestries hide in the dark alcoves, and above the fieldstone fireplace hangs a taxidermic triumph, still snarling at his old adversaries.

"Is that the legendary fox?"

"The farmers wanted to save the chickens and the ranchers needed coyotes dispatched to protect their calves, Horatio lived to eradicate the predator population. But killing them off just speeds up their reproduction. The Master didn't have much time for humans either. He said society was only attractive to deeply annoying people and being around them was just killing time."

"I see…," Alice said, but she really didn't. "Where did he get this curious mindset?"

"From the animals. People are never satisfied for long. They're always going to be happy 'someday.' The hounds don't have a time thing. They live in the here and now hunting, eating, and resting. Happiness is their way of being. A hound enjoys life as it happens."

"Speaking of enjoyment, do you ride?"

"I've ridden a mule in the Grand Canyon."

"Good, then you'll come hunting."

His radiant smile sweeps away Alice's objections, and she picks out 'a hunting we will go' from the few working keys on the dusty grand piano.

Two pensioned hounds push through a back door, amble across the room, and climb on the couch. "Napoleon and Caesar have the run of the house, they're too old to hunt."

"Looks like it's all going to the dogs."

"Never explain—never complain, that's what daddy said." Clayton takes the stack of mail off the desk and throws it in a wicker muck basket.

"Great filing system you've got there."

"Mostly bills I guess."

Alice picks a letter off the top, "This came special delivery and it's marked urgent."

Hatter looks away at the sleeping hounds.

"You had to sign for it and it's still sealed."

"I remember. The mailman made me sign but he can't make me read it."

"But…"

"A problem isn't a problem unless you think it's a problem… You read the mail if you'd like. I'll feed the horses."

Napoleon and Caesar slip off the couch and follow him out. Alice gathers up a dozen envelops and opens them at the desk. An hour, later Clayton returns and retreats upstairs. She hears the creaking steps and follows him. The musty rooms on the upper floors haven't seen daylight in years.

TOYS IN THE ATTIC

Alice opens the attic door and discovers an enormous playroom. A Cigar Store Indian stands guard at the threshold and giant chess pieces are scattered across the checkerboard floor.

Hatter sits at a long table with a battalion of toy soldiers and countless tubes of paint. "The Master kept these troops to fight his battles. They need constant attention… everything corrodes out here."

"Your accounts need some attending as well," she drops a handful mail next to a French Foreign Legionnaire.

"What's up? Just give me the highlights."

"It seems Horatio owed money to everyone in the Yellow Pages. Of course, the phone book won't be coming — Southern Bell shut off the service."

"The Master got tired of the telephone anyway, always someone wanting money. He was glad when they turned it off."

"Really?"

Kings, Queens, Knights, & Knaves Are Nestled Everywhere

"He wouldn't touch the phone or the mail. They gave him apoplexy. He said the Lord giveth and the Lord taketh away."

"Well, He's about to taketh away. You've got unpaid bills, back taxes, and a jumbo mortgage at First Florida Savings and Loan."

"That's Banker Coldwell, he always gave us money."

"It was a loan, not a gift. Your father put up nine of your twelve thousand acres as collateral."

"He mortgaged the chess board to keep playing the game."

Clayton stops painting and contemplates his predicament, "You mean we have to pay him back?"

Alice nods, "According to this statement you owe almost three million and its due in ninety days. Then there are back taxes. The IRS maintains Horatio never filed."

"I guess it's like the turn signals. He didn't get around to it. I should have burned those letters."

"This is impossible."

"Only if you believe it is."

"Why don't you just pay the bills?"

"There's no money." He picks up General Clemenceau and polishes his uniform.

"But the horses and hounds and all this hunting? Couldn't you give them something?"

"Think they'd take old Caesar?"

"I doubt it."

"There hasn't been a nickel around here since mother left. She was a Fair."

"A who?"

"Fair, Flood, O'Brien, and McKay— the Silver Kings discovered the Nevada

Comstock Load. Hildreth left us the farm and took the cash."

"Can't you sell some land to keep the alligators at bay?"

"No!" He bangs a toy cannon down on the table. "The Master might've borrowed against it, but you never sell hunt country. It's the beginning of the end."

"This will be the end of the end. Coldwell is ready to foreclose."

Clayton puts his arm around Alice. "What are our chances?"

She enjoys his touch for a moment, then pulls away. "You've got to pay the taxes and your mortgage."

"Easy for you to say. Where do we get the money?"

"Have you talked to Banker Coldwell?"

"Never… maybe you could talk to him?"

"I can, but what will you do now?"

"Now is the perpetual mystery. Guess I'll keep on hunting. I always eat my dessert first. There may not be room at the end."

"You better eat fast, before the bank takes your plate. Do you ever think of the future?"

"There is no future—just a perpetual present moment... You sound like an insurance salesman. I don't have to save up to get old and die."

"You're in denial."

"It works for me."

"With that attitude, what do you expect me to do?"

Anger flashes in Clayton's eyes, then sadness, "Nothing. In the end you'll only leave, just like mother."

"But I want to help."

"How?"

"Restore the place, make it attractive, and sell some land."

"I've never sold anything."

"I'm an agent at Land's End."

"What if some developer buys the place and builds another Century Village here?"

"There are risks, but if you take them yourself, the odds improve."

"Ramser won't go for it."

"Let him have the facts."

"Good, you tell him the plan. I only take orders, the Master made me read the instructions before I opened the Cheerios."

"I'll talk to Ramser."

"The artillery is in disarray… You're a determined little fox. I like that."

The constellation Centaurus shines down on the long-rutted driveway as Alice steers the old station wagon home. Her condo is sparsely furnished with white walls like the inside of a medicine cabinet. She's awakened by the Palm Beach Post striking the screen door. It's 7 o'clock—time for Good Morning America, and a Starbuck's double espresso. Alice is a pawn in the Land's End game and the hunt covers a very large chess board.

BANKER COLDWELL

In the mammoth lobby of the First Florida Savings and Loan, Alice asks a uniformed guard the whereabouts of Coldwell's office.

"Take the elevator down to the basement and turn left. He works in a vault at the end of the corridor."

The banker, wearing a grey pinstripe suit, rises to his full five feet and peers at Alice's business card through round, rimless spectacles. "Hmm, Land's End Development Company. That's Dolgin's outfit. Have a seat. I've dealt with Jordan before, he bought my Lantana Mall when it went belly up."

Alice surveys his crowded desk. Scrambled among the foreclosure notices are several complex horoscopes.

"I'm working out my astrological progressions." He slides the foreclosures into a drawer and takes out a leather-bound book. "You ought to read this Astro-Autobiography of Theophrastus von Hohenheim. He was the planetary physician who maintained that the stars force nothing on us that we are unable to take and incline us toward nothing that we do not desire."

The Black Forest clock chimes. A yellow bird emerges, spreads his wings and cuckoos ten times.

Alice is curious, "What can the planets tell me for sure?"

Coldwell moves his desk lamp toward her for a closer look. "You are a Capricorn and more interested in money than others might think or you would let on."

"What about love?"

"You have a karmic debt where romance is concerned. You failed to fulfill love's obligation in a previous incarnation and now you must double your efforts to achieve your goal... But what exactly are you doing here?"

"Everglades Hall..."

"So that's why you've come." He takes a deep breath and begins drawing dollar signs on a legal pad. "Old Horatio should be about ready to mortgage his last three thousand acres, and that land will be mine."

"But that's where they hunt."

"I couldn't care less about that Town and Country set. Horatio should've been retired to stud a long time ago."

"The Master won't need any more money. He's no longer with us."

"I see."

"What's going to happen to the land?"

"Foreclosure."

"But what about Clayton?"

"The lad will have to retreat with his soldiers. I've got three million lent out and nine thousand acres as collateral."

"But the place is worth ten times that."

"Land prices are supposed to go up. Whose side are you on anyway?"

The Cuckoo cackles again.

"I'd best be going, I'm late for work."

JORDAN DOLGIN

Alice parks the rusted station wagon in the Land's End lot. Dolgin watches from the window in his white flannel suit and twilight taupe tie—he looks like a Portobello smoking a cigar. Mushrooms have no chlorophyll. They are parasites in the vegetable kingdom.

Alice opens the door with a tentative wave, she rifles through the mail. The Boss smiles expecting a joke… No jest is forthcoming. "And what have you been up to?" Jordan is suspicious.

"I… I ran into a fox hunt. These dogs, I mean 'hounds' were chasing a rabbit across the road… I didn't hit them, but…"

"No!"

"The fenders and doors were demolished."

"Why'd I let you drive that car?"

"My Toyota is in the shop. Besides, you have a fleet of those antiques."

"A classic collection," Dolgin bites through his cigar and buries the remains in an overcrowded ashtray.

"Anyway, you own a large chunk of Eternity Federal, the Double Indemnity Insurance Company and the land under Acme Collision and Paint."

There's a knock on the door. Buzzy, the pint size gopher, brings the boss his Taco Bell combo breakfast and quickly takes his leave.

Dolgin grins, "Can't let anything spoil the first meal of the day." He raises a plastic fork in anticipation and dives into his huevos rancheros. "This foxing business, where do they do it?"

"Wellington and Loxahatchee, both sides of Southern Boulevard. They start at Everglades Hall."

"I know the place. Once tried to buy some land from a crazy old man in a red coat. I thought he was Santa Claus till he tried to run me over with his horse."

"Santa tried to jump your car and broke his neck."

"Think they'll sue?"

"No, Clayton has enough problems without a lawsuit."

"As I recall there are twelve thousand acres out there." He parcels out the land in his mind. "What's your angle?"

"We need some kindling to spark the Hall."

"It won't work. The insurance company won't buy that arson routine."

"We want five hundred thousand for three months to cheer up the house, and sell some land."

Dolgin does some quick calculations. "Here's what I can do. You can have the money for ninety days at sixteen percent. If you fail to repay the loan and interest, those last three thousand acres are mine."

He bows deferentially to a portrait of Washington covering the wall safe, then slides George back, spins the dial and listens to the tumblers click. The door swings open, and the old safecracker counts the cash into a shopping bag.

"Y'all should build a shopping center and make some real money."

"We want to preserve the land."

"What about progress and the great American way?"

"Clayton's American enough. He's into life, liberty and the pursuit of happiness."

"Has anyone told the lad the future's flying in."

"With all your mega-malls, there'll be no place to land."

"Malls are the future. Where else are folks gonna spend their weekends and their money?"

"They can go to the beach."

"Not healthy to lay out in those ultra-violet rays."

"Clayton wants to save the wildlife."

"That's the Metro Zoo's job. They feed the animals and clean their cages." Dolgin hands over a contract.

Alice signs.

"Congratulations on breaking the ice with the horsey set. Too bad old Hoopes broke his neck in the bargain."

As soon as she's out the door, Dolgin picks up the phone, "Yeah Mort, three thousand acres and we're talking the right stuff."

REST IN PEACE

The Master's funeral is well underway when Alice arrives at St. Edwards. Horatio is laid out in an open casket. He died and will be buried with his boots on. She is drawn to the last row, genuflects, trying to conceal the shopping bag, and sits down next to a lady who bears a curious resemblance to Clayton.

Hildreth Hoopes is incognito in a broad-brimmed hat and sunglasses. "The Master was notorious in here. Our pew was right behind the Kennedy's. Every Sunday, when Horatio rustled through his newspapers, Rose would turn around and glare, but he took no notice."

The eulogy drones on, "Somehow it is his defiance, and whole-hearted dedication to living his unique life that must be Horatio's redemption… Had he lived beyond his threescore years and ten, there might have been some autumnal mellowing in the Master's character…."

Hildreth leans in toward Alice, "As it is, he goes to his grave unreformed and unrepentant. It would be unchristian of me to be glad Mr. Hoopes is no longer with us, but damned if I know what purpose he served alive. Well, he's God's problem now."

The parishioners stand and sing, "Faith of our fathers living still, in spite of dungeon fire and sword…"

Hildreth rises to leave before the hymn's conclusion, "If you run into trouble dear, come see me. I've dropped anchor near the Flagler, but don't tell anyone I'm in town."

As the congregation files out, Clayton comes into view. "The Master's gone to ground and we're off to lunch with the hunt committee."

charley's crab®

At a back table, in celebration of the Jabberwock's life, Ramser, Victoria, and Bruno are inhaling vodka martinis and extracting Dungeness crabs from their claws. The Pillar proposes a toast, "Foxhunters everywhere will long remember the late Master and how he passed on in pursuit of the hounds he loved. It is for us, the living, to uphold his traditions and we here highly resolve that Foxhunting shall not perish from Palm Beach."

"That's a fine rehash of Gettysburg's address," Victoria's unsentimental sentiments.

"Then let's get on with it, I would like to put before the committee an offer to fill the late Master's boots."

"Hear, hear," Bruno seconds the motion.

The Queen Victoria objects, "Hold on, why not make me Master? I'm a born ruler and well-versed in hunting etiquette. Or, by rights, the honor should go to Clayton."

The Pillar menacingly turns toward the Hatter, "Do you have any objections?"

"I haven't given the matter any thought."

"Good, then it's settled. Thank you, one and all."

Bruno utters an urgent plea, "I need money for kennel rations. The hounds are scavenging the countryside for food and while this is a noble conservation effort, there are drawbacks. Old Hercules was dognapped by a redneck and Rumbler was run over by a snow bird."

Ramser concurs, "The Huntsman's point is well taken, but I regret to report our coffers are empty. Can we hear from the social committee?"

Victoria is ready. "The Hunt Ball is almost upon us. This year's theme is a Lobster Quadrille, Lester Lanin and his Royal Floridians will supply the music."

Ramser recoils, "Sounds rather pricey."

"I'll pay the musicians."

"Let's get on with it," Ramser repeats. "What about the races, Clayton?"

"I'm planning an old fashion point-to-point. We'll start at Lion Country Safari and race seven miles east to Everglades Hall. Of course, we are still looking for a sponsor… Which brings me to another matter, if we all wish to continue hunting with hounds, we must raise some cash. The situation is bleak, but there is hope."

He looks at Alice for inspiration and continues, "We have in our midst a financial Pied Piper who can dispel our creditors and restore our funds."

"Humbug" says Bruno.

The introduction takes Alice by surprise. She stands up quickly hoping to think faster on her feet. "This is going to be a hard sell so I'll keep it short. I've gone over your records, such as they are, and the IRS, Banker Coldwell, and a gaggle of vendors all want their money. Your only hope is to sell some remaining land and bail out the Hunt country and Everglades Hall in one fell swoop."

"Swoop indeed." Ramser is irate. "Foxhunting is a sport, not a commercial enterprise. It's hard enough to ride horses verging on heat prostration following hounds paddling through alligator infested canals, chasing a diminishing number of foxes through sweltering swamps without some land-grabbing developer littering the landscape with prefab bungalows and all the attending flotsam and jetsam."

"Right on!" Bruno chimes in.

Ramser's rants on, "Besides I don't cotton to carpetbaggers coming down here changing things. And one more thing young lady, don't take advantage of Clayton's disheartening dilemma."

Alice is furious, "I don't know where you're coming from, but the trains don't go there anymore."

"Listen to me…"

"Hunt your heart out, till the land's foreclosed and you're hauled off for trespassing."

"Outsiders! We can't turn this hunt over to outsiders."

Clayton stands up, "Outsiders, insiders, what's the difference? We need to find some people with deep pockets."

Victoria adds, "For the last decade, the Pillar has blackballed every proposed new member."

Ramser backs off, "If you have a plan, let's hear it."

Alice produces the shopping bag and empties the money on the table. "There's five-hundred-thousand here."

Charlie's Crab starts to buzz, and Ramser's incredulity makes her day.

"We have three months to restore the place up and sell enough land to pay off the mortgage and the taxes."

"If you fail to find a buyer, this money will be considered a donation to the hound fund." Ramser drives a hard bargain. "And you better bank that cash before you lose it."

Clayton nominates Alice for treasurer with full hunting privileges.

Victoria seconds the motion and offers congratulations, "Glad you're joining the hunt. Tomorrow we'll shop for your habit."

The meeting adjourns.

"Do you really think we can save the land?" The Hatter still isn't sure.

"It can be saved, but it will take some resolve."

Since mother left, "I don't make decisions—decisions make me."

"Do you miss her?"

He brushes away a tear, "Yes, I miss them both, but the Master hated displays of emotion."

She wants to tell him about Hildreth, but knows she mustn't.

GUCCI

WORTH AVENUE

Victoria and Alice are sitting in the back of the yellow Rolls-Royce. Eames is driving in the middle of South Ocean Boulevard. Fortunately, Worth Avenue is just one block away.

"Let's start at Gucci, they have nice boots."

"I bet they're expensive."

"In the hunt field, appearances are everything, it's polite to have money or at least to look like you do."

Eames parks in front and lets the ladies out. Alice looks through the Italian loafers and red velvet sneakers, and finally finds a pair of black riding boots.

A smiling, narrow hipped, Euro salesman comes forward. "Most of our clients shop for the loafers, but we do have boots and whips for the more adventuresome."

Alice sits down in a wingback chair. Euro supplies a pair of boot hooks and watches her struggle into the new leather.

"A perfect fit! Good thing, too. They're the only pair in stock, we don't do a roaring trade in riding gear."

She looks at the price tag for the first time. "At three thousand a pair, I can understand why."

The salesman quotes Aldo Gucci, "Quality is remembered long after price is forgotten."

She wriggles out of the boots, happy to feel her circulation returning.

Eames carefully places the purchase in the trunk and drives on to Hermes, where a nattily attired Monsieur Theil greets them at the door.

The Red Queen brandishes several white silk scarfs. "The stock is de riguer, it makes an elegant sling if you break your arm, and a useful tourniquet, should your horse sever and artery."

Alice wonders what she would do with an uber-expensive blood-soaked silk scarf.

Theil herds them toward the rear of the store. "At one time Hermes sold all the equipage to the Parisian carriage trade. That was back in the day when they arrived in carriages."

Victoria pulls a yellow lap robe off a sidesaddle. "Let's have a look."

The salesman carefully places the tack on an antique carousel horse, "To my mind a woman riding aside has every credential a lady requires. The practice traces back to 1382, when Princess Anne of Bohemia rode sidesaddle across Europe on her way to marry King Richard II."

He gives Alice a leg-up and arranges her legs around the leaping horns. "It's the easiest thing in the world my dear, and really quite safe."

She sits up straight and a tingle of delight races through her thighs. "I'll take it."

Theil adds up the damage at the register, "One sidesaddle, a navy blue gabardine habit, and two silk scarfs. That will be seven thousand, seven hundred and seventy-six dollars."

Victoria hands him a Gold American Express Card.

Eames purposefully piles the package next to the boots.

"Let's eat at Petite Marmite. Eames won't have to move the car."

Victoria jaywalks across Worth Avenue with Alice in tow. They settle at a window table. "I'll have the calves' brains in black butter with capers, and the kidneys in mustard sauce for my friend, and a bottle of your Châteauneuf-du-Pape."

Alice is thankful for the wine to wash down the kidneys.

"How are you and Clayton getting along?"

"It's not easy. Sometimes he's in the attic crusading with the troops and other times he's in other realms."

"There was no 'there there' with Horatio. And he got his 'somewhere else' when Hildreth sailed away. With his short attention span, he couldn't sit still in school so he played hooky. The phone was off the hook and no one opened the mail—Saint Andrew's Prep gave up."

"It's all so odd."

"Of course, the Master couldn't keep a groom, so he wanted his son in the stable. The horses came straight from Hialeah and Clayton hunted them right out of the box. He never had a failure with a horse or a success with a human being. Horses meant freedom, he doesn't really trust people… He loves blasts of novelty, but fears abandonment, so he always jumps ship first.

When Hildreth left, Horatio lost the string to his kite. He kept spending money, but his heart just wasn't in it anymore."

Alice looks distressed.

"It wasn't your fault. It seems the Master got out just in time. We're all waiting for Clayton's ship to come in, but with Ramser at the helm, it might sink. Reginald spent thirty years in the Marines. The Generals pointed to the enemy and he made short work of them. Trouble is, now he can't tell friend from foe, plus he doesn't know what a good time is, much less how to have one."

The waiter arrives with Champagne, "Compliments of Señor Mendoza."

"Ask the gentleman to join us." Victoria smiles, "He's a rich Argentinean with a fleet of planes and a herd of world-class polo ponies."

Merlos sits down, "Buen Provecho ladies."

The waiter fills their glasses and Victoria launches into their plight. "We are trying to save our hunt country."

"Your country?" Merlos looks out the window.

"There are twelve thousand acres out behind Wellington and the bank is about to foreclose on most of them. We need to sell what's left."

"Is this a good investment?"

"The best. There are three thousand acres where you can land your planes and stable your horses."

"I must look into this. Argentina is changing regimes again. It might be the moment to move some assets to Florida."

"There's not much time."

Merlos glances at his watch. "In America time flies, but I must go. Fifteen minutes late for polo and we forfeit the game." He bows to Alice, throws a kiss to Victoria. A moment later his Maserati roars down Worth Avenue.

"Merlos has the land speed record for the twelve miles to Wellington."

Alice is intrigued. "He's a hot prospect. What does he do with the planes?"

"He flies stuff to South America."

"Stuff?"

"Cigarettes, Bourbon, Levis… you know, contraband. He calls himself the Troposphere Express."

"Contraband Levis?"

"Sure, jeans are a big item. Twelve bucks a pair at the factory, a hundred on the streets of Buenos Aires."

"Is that legal?"

"It's all legally purchased and shipped. It isn't contraband till the plane lands."

"What does he bring back?"

"He manufactures saddles in Argentina. He's a good contact. Keeping my house on the ocean is expensive, new money maintains the old traditions."

A HUNTING WE
WILL GO

Alice has rounded up Dolgin's contractors and refurbished Everglades Hall. The brick facade is restored, the fences painted, and the hunt is gathering on a freshly manicured lawn. Loxahatchee Lil wasn't quite sound coming out of her stall. Upon closer inspection, she's missing a shoe and Clayton is reluctantly missing the hunt.

Alice is decked out sidesaddle in her new habit. Clyde is pawing the ground and grinding his teeth without a stablemate.

Iona and Dick Wickstrom, a hard of hearing couple, pull up at the last minute in their Jeep and two-horse trailer.

"It costs nothing to be on time." Ramser critically points to his watch.

"One minute Master, we'll be right with you." Iona calls, as their horses clamor down the ramp.

Bruno scolds the hounds, "Pack in now have a care," Persnickety, a young entry, wanders off. The Huntsman cracks his whip and without warning, Clyde pops his cork and careens through the pack. Alice struggles to hold her stirrup cup and her horse.

Ramser is irate, "For God's sake, drop your drink and pick up the reins... Horatio always rode Clyde up front, but I trust you'll keep him in the back."

Snatching the reins and gripping the leaping horns, she finally gets her horse under control and ends up next to Victoria.

"How do you get your horse to stand still?"

"Every time he moves I hit him."

The hunt moves off, and Alice falls in with the Wickstroms for shelter.

"I'm Iona and this is my husband Dick," The loyal members are already sweating in their black melton coats, and she is cramming her Brillo grey hair under a bowler. "I need a safe little horse. At my age, coming home alive is half the fun."

Without warning, Clyde flattens his ears and attacks Iona's palomino pony.

Ramser taps his boot with his whip, "Remember no smoking in the woods or chatting at the checks."

Clyde whinnies impatiently.

A gray fox saunters out of the gazebo and trots across the lawn.

"Tally-Ho," shouts Iona, the hounds are on it, and they're off.

Clyde's ears shoot forward and his stride becomes electric. Alice finds herself galloping along in the first flight, her sidesaddle skirts billowing in the wind. A four-rail fence looms ahead. Trying to turn to no avail, she grabs the mane and closes her eyes.

Her horse stands well back and easily clears the jump.

The second fence looks less ominous and by the third, her fear of flying has vanished. The fox is leading them on a merry chase and the hounds are in full cry.

Suddenly a dark shadow falls over the field and the roar of rotors scatters the hounds. Frightened horses go to squealing and bucking, depositing their flabbergasted riders on the ground.

"Dick! Dick! Dick!" Iona screams and falls off. Mr. Wickstrom has also come a cropper and is wandering about with his top hat driven down over both ears.

Mort Waldorf emerges from his helicopter, oblivious to the havoc, smiling and wearing a bright red leisure suit. "My name's Mort. I've come to meet all you nice people and look at the land you have for sale. Can anyone direct me to Alice Liddell?"

Alice is still hooked aboard Clyde and grimacing at the mention of her name.

Ramser is beside himself. "Let's get on with it."

Bruno calls the hounds, "Come away, leave it." The hounds pack up and the huntsman casts them in another direction trying to retrieve the quarry's scent.

The ball is in Alice's court. She dismounts, ties Clyde's reins to the copter's landing gear, and confronts the Red King. "What can I do for you?"

"Looks like a well-stocked pond. Has anyone else been out to fish?"

"You're the first."

There's a thud as Clyde digs in and pulls back against the landing gear. His reins are tangled in the tail rotor and Alice wades into the fray.

Mort carefully keeps his distance. "West Palm is growing fast, but there's room to expand out here…"

There's another crash as Clyde puts a hoof through the whirlybird's aluminum body.

Waldorf ignores the carnage. "My Wonderland Country Club will fit in nicely… Where's this Clayton Hoopes anyway?"

"He's at home." Alice flinches as Clyde kicks the copter again. "I'd like to discuss this further, but the horse is agitated and we don't want to miss the hunt." She unties the reins, climbs on the fender, and swings onto the saddle.

The palm trees merge in a brilliant blur as Clyde races off in search of the hounds. Caught up in the momentum, Alice fails to notice a six-strand barbed wire gate looming in her path. The cattle stop grazing to watch the action. At the last minute, she sees the wire. "Go for it," she grabs the mane anticipating another euphoric launch.

Clyde doesn't like the look of the barbs and stops dead in his tracks. Alice flies over the gate alone and lands in a nest of Bermuda grass. The horse surveys the situation, turns on his haunches and gallops off.

She recalls Monsieur Theil's words, "Easiest thing in the world, and really quite safe." What would he know anyway?

Her sandwich case was torn from the saddle and is close at hand. She removes a ham sandwich and the small flask of sherry. Bayard, the lead hound appears and wanders over.

"You lost too fella?" she scratches his ears. The hound looks longingly at the sandwich. She feeds it to him, finishes off the sherry and gets to her feet, "Let's go home."

Bayard lays down.

"Come along then, lieu-in, lieu-in." Alice is a quick study, but to no avail, there's not much a neophyte foxhunter can tell a seasoned hound. She strikes out along the fence line, with Bayard tagging along. "Did Clyde find his way back, is Clayton worried? They'll surely come looking for you, won't they?"

After an hour, the landscape begins to look familiar. The kennels are just ahead. Bayard gets his bearing and runs forward to join his mates. Alice opens the gate cautiously and tries to slip the hound in. Without warning the whole pack barges through the gap, knocking her to the ground. The hounds tear across the field. Only her new friend remains behind.

Bruno appears in a cloud of dust, enraged at the retreating pack and wielding his whip, "Mettlesome wench, Carpetbagger. First your damned fool friend ruins the hunt with his chopper and now you're letting these varmints out. You think I like chasing them over hell's half acres?" The Huntsman cracks his whip menacingly. Alice ducks away. Bayard growls at Bruno who whacks him with the handle.

"Stop that." Alice springs into action, grabs the rotund huntsman by his coattails and spins him into the fence. The thong wraps around his ankles, he staggers and falls.

Bruno The Bandersnatch with blood in his eye

Grabs for Alice, who starts to cry,

And tries to avoid the way of harm

But The Huntsman extends his arm

And grabs for Alice again.

Then without a pause—those frumious jaws

Go savagely snapping around—

Tally Ho

He jumps and hops and flounders and flops,

And stumbles and falls to the ground.

She makes her escape, dashing across the yard into the old red barn and climbing a rickety ladder up to the hayloft.

"Come out and die like a man you land grabbing coward."

Bruno pursues her with a pitchfork, jabs it into the straw, and then takes a stab in the oat bin. "I'll feed you to the hounds." He starts up the ladder with Bayard snapping at his heels.

Alice is cowering in a corner of the loft. It won't be long now. She crawls over to a trap door, looks down and sees Gryphon the huntsman's horse still saddled and munching alfalfa in his stall.

"Now I've got you," The furious Bandersnatch reaches for her throat.

She screams, jumps down through the opening, and lands on the startled horse, who breaks through his stall guard and races out of the barn. She finds her stirrups and gets her bearings. Gryphon is clearly tired galloping along the Homeland trail, but the old campaigner will still carry the mail.

Alice hears the sound of a straining engine. She searches the sky for the chopper and then looks back. Bruno is chasing them in the hound truck, albeit stuck in first gear.

"Help!" She bends low on the horse's neck and urges him into the underbrush. The truck is on their tail rattling over cabbage palms and careening through the ditches.

Everglades Hall comes into view. Alice gallops across the ornamental bridge certain that Bruno won't follow. Safe on the other side she pulls up. But the enraged huntsman drives onto the bridge knocking the railings apart. The span gives way and the truck plunges into the pond. After a moment, Bruno floats to the surface and dog-paddles his way to the shore.

Clayton speeds down the driveway with Waldorf in the passenger seat.

"Thank God…" Alice dismounts and falls into his arms.

Mort looks at the submerged truck and the drenched huntsman on the bank. "You're all mad. Catch you later." The King of Hearts zips up his leisure suit and dashes for his helicopter like Chicken Little escaping the falling sky.

Clayton laughs as the whirlybird roars skyward. "He wants to turn this place into an Equestrian Disneyland. That won't sit well with Ramser. I was worried when Clyde came back alone, what happened anyway?"

She points to Bruno still trying to catch his breath, "It's a long story."

The Huntsman gets up with a hangdog look and slinks off to call a wrecker. They lead Gryphon to the stable, hose him off, and turn him out.

"These boots are killing me."

Clayton sits Alice down on the tack room's mule hide sofa and straddles a boot. "Now push with the other."

"Like that?" She gives it a try.

"Harder."

She plants her foot firmly on his bottom and sends him flying across the room.

"That's more like it." The second boot comes off with far less exertion and they celebrate with a snifter of brandy.

Horatio never paid much attention to the house but the tack room is filled with generations of meticulously polished heirloom leather. Clayton fills a bucket with warm water, kneads a bar of glycerin soap until sponge begins to foam, and carefully removes the sweat stains from Alice's boots.

"Looks like you have more than a passing interest in leather."

He stands behind her and gently rubs her shoulders in a slow sensuous rhythm as she attaches a burnished iron to a pliant leather.

THE HUNT BALL

The full moon's silver beams illuminate the Hall's crenelated towers. Eames is parking cars as guests arrive for the Lobster Quadrille. The foxhunters are stalking an evening of fun, food, and gossip. Ladies are regaled in black and white bejeweled gowns and gentlemen in scarlet tails. Polo players and their dates spill out of new dual-wheel pickups and sleek Porsches to be greeted by Morals dispensing Champagne in a blue-and-white striped tent.

Merlos Mendoza is accompanied by his daughter GoGo, a sexy twenty-something wearing an emerald green dress that's translucent under the lights. She watches distractedly as a foursome of fellow players slip behind the tent, emerging moments later with sparkling eyes and quivering nostrils. As the Royal Floridian's refrains drift over the lawn, GoGo catches Clayton's hand and leads him to the dance floor.

Victoria observes, "Really can't blame her, men and horses are God's premier creations."

"She goes through her share." Merlos adds. He notices Alice's distress and presents her with glass of champagne. She swallows it down and wanders toward the ballroom where GoGo's gyrations are driving the more sedentary dancers to the edge of the floor.

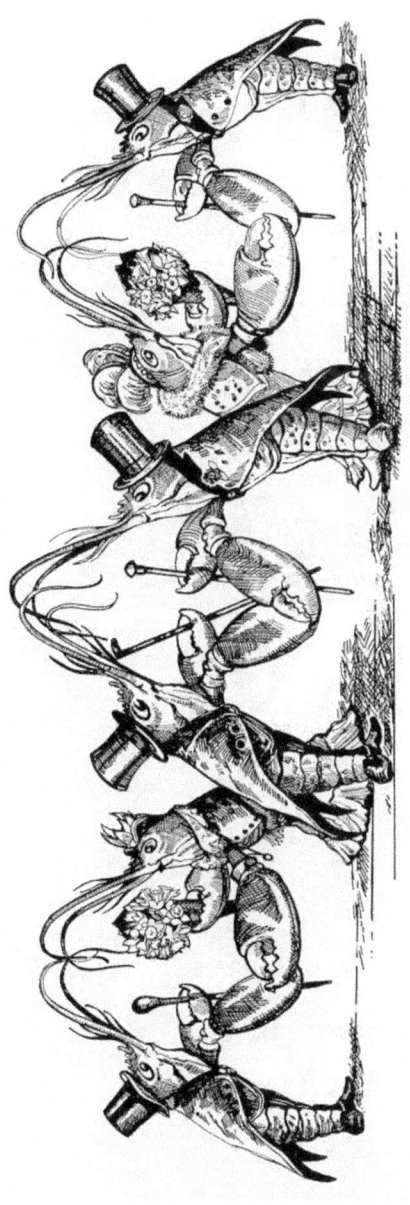

DOING THE LOBSTER-QUADRILLE

Martin Blunt
https://www.flickr.com/photos/mbpencils

*Can you a dance a little faster said Miss GoGo -
there's a whale*

*Of a Huntsman close behind us and he's treading
on my tail*

See how eagerly the turtles and the lobsters all advance

*Will you, won't you, will you won't you, will you
speed up the dance?*

*Will you, won't you, will you won't you, won't
you speed up the dance?*

You really have no notion how delightful it will be

Twirling round much faster in delightful company.

A big bass drum booms, and the band strikes up Hail to the Chief. Alice follows the gaze of the assembled guests to the foyer where Jordan Dolgin is making a grand entrance with his glittering tails and a top hat—he looks like Thaddeus Toad. The crowd stands transfixed.

"I read about your little shindig in the papers," Dolgin announces.

Alice reluctantly walks over to greet the boss, "Glad you could come."

She offers to take his hat, but he tosses it on the medieval knight's helmet and heads for the bar.

"Jack Daniels, straight up, my good man."

The bartender smiles, "Sorry sir… we don't have…"

Dolgin is incensed, "Can't believe there's no Tennessee whiskey."

He settles for a shot of Old Crow and trundles off to sample the pâté at the banquet tables. "A lot of pigs and turkeys died to be here tonight."

Dolgin shoulders his way past Bruno wearing a well-worn tuxedo, "What have we here and in tails no less?"

"Lands' End Inc. Can I help you?" Dolgin's feathers are ruffled.

A small crowd gathers around the adversaries.

Ramser steps between the ham and turkey and glares at Alice, "How dare you invite him?"

Dolgin recognizes his old schoolmate, "Why, it's Reginald Ramski, Prince of Poland High, the skinny kid who ran home after school to play with his hang-ups."

"Toad… What the Hell are you doing here?"

"Watching you ride your high-horse."

Ramser goes ballistic, "I'll high-horse you right out the door."

Dolgin brandishes a hambone.

Alice looks around for a referee — Bruno Mangus, defender of the stars, to the rescue.

While washing down the remains of a ham sandwich with a tumbler of Burgundy, the Huntsman attempts to block for Ramser. "Show the Master a little respect. You know, some noblesse oblige."

"Master my…" A drumroll drowns out Dolgin's tail end.

Bruno grabs the makeshift weapon and inadvertently spills red wine all over Dolgin's white dress shirt.

The Toad leaps around like a wild boar in a vat of boiling vinegar, "You'll pay for this, when I get my hands on this land, you'll be hunting in hell." He bolts for the door and stalks out into the gathering storm.

Ramser growls at Alice, "What have you done? First, we're besieged by Waldorf and his helicopter, and now here's the Toad on our backs. What was he doing here anyway?"

"Checking up on his money."

"His money…? You don't mean…?"

"Who do you think would bail you out, the Easter Bunny?"

"And now, what?"

In floods of tears Alice runs out into the rain. Clayton is off somewhere with GoGo, Dolgin has disrupted the ball, and Dom Perignon is producing an untimely hangover. She finds refuge in her car, closes her eyes, and is assailed by a nightmare revelation.

The Four Horsemen of the Apocalypse
Gallop Through the Gloom.

Horatio carries a tomahawk and rides a black horse galloping on the heels of the Devil Fox. Bruno follows on a fiery red roan with large iron teeth and eleven horns. At his side is Cerberus, the massive, three-headed black hound that guards the entrance to Hades. Ramser, on a white horse is a harbinger of the final destruction. Saturiba chases after them riding a deadly pale steed. The Chief is holding a set of scales to weigh the hunters' fate.

Alice shudders at the final revelation when a clap of thunder jolts her awake. The four horsemen disappear in the night sky and are replaced by a sailboat and the memory of Hildreth's words, "If you run into trouble dear, come and see me."

SERENDIPITY

The next afternoon, Alice is walking along the Lake Worth trail toward the Flagler Museum, when a dachshund scuttles by and runs up the SeaScape's gang-plank.

Hildreth smiles, "Sorry about Serendipity, he's always in a hurry. Would you care to come aboard for tea?"

The boat rocks gently and Alice relaxes away from Land's End and the Hunt's tribulations.

SERENDIPITY

The seafarer wears a silver albatross on her necklace and like the Ancient Mariner, she must tell her tale. "That fiendish man with his infernal hunt. He turned paradise into hell. He had land aplenty and could ride where he pleased. His only admonition was not to disturb the Seminole burial ground, but Horatio could not resist evil. He killed a fox in the consecrated ground with the Chiefs own tomahawk. The Medicine Man said the weapon was interred to protect Saturiba's journey to the happy hunting ground. Of course,

Horatio gave the ax to Clayton and hung the fox over the fireplace."

Alice recalled the ghastly trophy.

"Stone Bear put a curse on Horatio. At first, the Master experienced a new vitality—a little arsenic will do that for a horse—but there was a restlessness in his soul that set him apart. He bought land and built fences way beyond his needs and was immune to the suffering of others. He became the quintessential unspeakable in the pursuit of the eminently inedible."

"Clayton never really bonded with either of us. He processed his emotions talking to the hounds. As a child, he knew all their names and walked the pack out by himself. He fed the horses and rode every day. The animals were always happy to see him. He belonged and believed in the relationships that worked. Of course, it was all a bit odd, he would canter around the house and bark when strangers came to the door. His father thought it was funny. Guess I should have taken more notice."

"That's when you left?"

"Growing up sailing, the water was my sanctuary. I couldn't stay. I knew early on this marriage was a mistake. The accountants told me to get out while I could. My psychiatrist was leaving town and suggested I do the same."

"What about Clayton?"

"He was only eleven at the time. Riding and hunting was all the fun a boy could have. I couldn't take him away from everything he loved."

"But now he's bogged down in debt, you can help."

"He'll only stumble into the quicksand down the road. Money's not the answer. Saturiba's curse must be undone."

Alice stares at a portrait of the Seminole chief smoking a peace pipe.

"You're in love with Clayton, the horses, and those scarlet coats. I sailed into The Master's port and never paid attention to the rocks."

"He deserves a chance…"

"Our only chance is the one we take ourselves. Why don't you go to the Reservation and find the Medicine Man? Now, with Horatio gone, perhaps he can lift the curse."

WITH RESERVATIONS

Alligator Alley runs between the Everglades tropical wetlands and the waters of the Big Cypress Swamp where Ghost orchids and invasive pythons are concealed from the passing traffic. Alice drives through a Panther Wildlife Refuge and finally arrives at the Big Cypress Reservation, a vast wilderness inhabited by the Seminole tribes and vast herds of cattle. She turns her Toyota onto a dirt road lined with palmetto thatched huts.

"Tourist?" The squaw is washing her clothes in front of a chickee.

"No, I'm looking for Stone Bear, the medicine man."

"Funny old shaman…"

"Where can I find him?"

"Stone Bear died last month, death was unexpected, no one could save him."

"What did he die of?"

"Not sick, just died."

"Can I talk to the Chief?"

"Chief is in Tallahassee lobbying against new highway."

"Is there another Medicine Man?"

"White Eagle is gone to Miami, for prostate operation."

"Is there anyone here who can help me with a curse?"

"I hope not. It's bad to call up evil spirits." The old Squaw collects her laundry and slips into her hut.

Alice drives on. The town is one long block out of the Ozark's circa 1947. The old Texaco station still has hi-test pumps and a broken-down grease rack surrounded by acres of junk cars. The dilapidated movie theater houses a post office. She opens the screen door of the Anhinga Trading Post. Kicking Crawfish, a young brave in black jeans and a fringed cowboy shirt leans against the refrigerated case drinking a YooHoo.

"Hi," Alice reaches for a chocolate favored drink. "I need someone to lift a curse?"

"I'm a rain dancer, bring water from the sky."

"Could you try? Stone Bear put the curse of Saturiba on Horatio Hoopes, now they're both dead."

"Sometimes enemies die together. Stone Bear made powerful magic." Crawfish swallows the last of his drink, "Bring six cartons of Kools, a case of Bacardi, and a color TV, then I'll give it a try."

"A color television?"

"The Hopis foretold a magic box would sit in a corner, we would see people from far away."

Alice's takes her best shot, "All right, it's a deal."

Driving back through Hialeah she comes upon a well-lit Big Daddy's Liquor store. Big D himself is at the register.

"Where can I find the rum?"

"Aisle 5."

There are a dozen brands, with various hues, Captain Morgan has an elaborate display.

"Is this rum any good?"

"Second largest selling brand in the US and seventh worldwide. It's on sale this week."

"I'll take a case."

"They'll be whooping it up on the reservation tonight."

"I hope not." She heads for the register. "And I want six cartons of Kools."

"We're out of Kools. How about Camels?"

"Camels will be fine."

"Having a party? I hate to pass up an invitation, if one's in the offing."

Alice shakes her head no and wheels a heavily laden shopping cart out to her car.

Once home, she stares doggedly at her 17-inch television, pulls the plug and wraps the cord around the rabbit ears. Time is of the essence so she drives all the way back to the Reservation and leaves the ransom on the trading post porch.

Getting home in dawn's early light, there's a message on her answering machine. Clients from Texas are flying in tomorrow morning.

THE COOPERS

Tropical storm Hope is flooding the Palm Beaches and washing out sections of A1-A. Alice arrives at the American Airlines Terminal just as Rex and Dale Cooper come through the revolving doors. The tall Texans are decked out from hat to boots by Ralph Lauren and followed by a porter juggling six matching green lizard suitcases. Lone Star, their oversized Afghan Hound, prances alongside Dale. Just as Alice gets out to greet them, the Afghan races into the road and is nearly run over by an air-port bus.

Rex is quick to explain, "The dog is neurotic on a leash, and Dale humors him."

The porter piles the suit cases in the trunk. Dale and Lone Star get in back. Rex rides shotgun for the short drive to Wellington.

Dale is a fast talker, "We made our money in Midland oil and moved to Dallas where the people are more cosmopolitan, but the winters are freezing. It's hard on the horses and the cattle and all the nice people who work for us. So, when we saw the ad for Everglades Hall, what with the hunting and all that land, we had to take a look."

They stop at a light next to an old Dodge pickup driven by a good old boy wearing a red plastic 'Make America

Great' cap and drinking an Old Milwaukee. Lone Star spots a pit bull in the truck bed and lunges half way out the window growling ferociously. Dale shouts and hauls the dog back.

Alice suggests, "You might want to check in at the Hyatt and find a kennel."

"No siree," Dale vetoes the idea. "Let's go right out to the hunt country. Do they really have alligators down here?"

"We sure do, you can spot them on the golf course."

"The only gators I've seen were on Rex's shorts." Dale laughs, "And real fox hunts, just like in the movies? Can't wait to see where they do it."

Alice looks plaintively at Rex.

"Once the little lady gets an idea in her head, that's pretty much it."

They drive to some remote hunt country in Bink's Woods and admire a bunch of chicken coop jumps laid over the barbed wire.

"Just like old Virginia." Alice keeps heading out along the canals, which all look the same… until they're lost.

Lone Star is bored and half napping. Suddenly his ears go up. A white rabbit is making his way along the other side of the canal. The hound jumps from the moving car and swims across the water in hot pursuit.

Rex cheers him on, "Look at the son-ver-bitch go! The Easter bunny doesn't stand a chance."

"Stop, Lone Star, come back." Dale is overwrought, "Turn this thing around, please. The alligators."

LONE STAR

The canal road is one sandy lane. Alice slows down for a U-turn in the under-brush. One-third of the way around, the ground gives way. The wheels spin and they are dug-in up to the fenders. Two taps on the accelerator and the engine conks out.

"Are we stuck?" Dale inquires.

"Don't ask," replies Rex.

The skies open, Dale jumps out of the car in the downpour and sprints back along the canal.

"The Mrs. gets like this from time to time." Her husband takes off struggling through the sand in his Tony Lama boots, Alice follows.

Dale is out of breath, "How will we ever find the poor thing?"

"If that hound has a nickel's worth of brains he'll come back."

They finally come upon Lone Star sprawled out in a stand of melaleucas. The rabbit is long gone. The trek back in the pouring rain is interrupted by an approaching truck.

"Maybe the good old boy's coming back to fish," Rex is hopeful.

The hound truck comes into view. Bruno is driving. Clayton, Victoria, and Ramser climb out.

Alice makes the introductions, "The Coopers hail from Texas. They're shopping for land."

Rex starts to shake hands, "Howdy Mr. Ramser. We're thinking about raising some cattle in these parts."

Ramser looks skeptically at the western boots and the cowboy suits, "Cows and more wire fences, just what we need."

"How nice for us," Rex recoils.

Clayton tries to move the conversation in a neutral direction. "We're mapping out the course for our upcoming steeple-chase."

"Lucky we came along, when we did." Victoria finds the new cowboy attractive. "Those cute little cows and, mmm… Got Milk?"

Dale is exasperated. "We raise Herefords for beef."

Bruno perks up at the mention of meat, "Raising cattle down here is a swell idea Mrs. Cooper, Filet Mignon is my very favorite comestible."

Rex points out, "There's more to the cattle than filets."

"That's okay, we can throw the rest to the hounds." The Huntsman's suggestion doesn't sit well.

Rex turns to Dale, "Texas winters are easier to take than these foxhunters."

It's still raining Sunday evening, as the Country Squire pulls up to the Terminal. Clayton and Alice are in front, Rex, Dale, and Lone Star are in the back. There is some semblance of civility as goodbyes are said, and the Texans, the Afghan, and the luggage all head back to Big D.

Alice is discouraged, "Between Ramser's enthusiasm and Bruno's brilliant ideas we don't stand a chance. Time is running out."

Clayton adds, "And I still don't have a sponsor. All this rain won't help."

LANDS END

Alice is at her desk. Dolgin is puffing on a cigar and pacing the floor. "Your swell friends didn't give Waldorf much of a welcome."

"Landing his helicopter on the hounds didn't help."

"He'll be back. Anyone else looking at the Hall?"

"The Coopers flew up from Texas."

"I suppose Ramser ran them off… How's that boyfriend of yours? I hear he's a pocket of loose change."

Alice is distraught, "Clayton's looking for someone to sponsor the steeplechase. It brings in hordes of spectators."

"I read about the race in the Post, it's an annual fixture of sorts."

"We need a backer."

Dolgin tries to make amends, "Racing's my game—Gulf-stream, Tropical Park—how much are they running for?"

"There no purse, they race for the thrill of it."

"That's got to be revised. How much do you need?"

"The course has to be built and the media alerted."

Dolgin takes a pie from a small refrigerator under his desk, "Nothing like mile high key lime pie." He cuts himself an ample slice of the quivering confection and inhales every gelatinous morsel. "Tell you what, I'll sponsor the race myself and there'll be ten thousand Land's End dollars for the winner."

"You will?"

Dolgin scans the ceiling like an outfielder waiting for a fly ball. "Sure, Waldorf's construction company can build the jumps and I'll take care of the rest."

"You'll do all that?"

"In for a dime, in for a dollar. Besides it'll be worth it to see you race."

"Me race?"

"You'll be another National Velvet."

"What's in it for you? Philanthropy isn't your pastime."

"A sporty fling, a little good will, maybe even make amends with Ramski."

"None of the above, but it's an offer I can't refuse."

"Today, the Point to Point, tomorrow the Derby."

STABLES

Clayton's denim shirt is covered with horsehair. He's fully absorbed clipping his mare and only looks up when Serena's shadow falls across the horse.

Alice notices how she stands without being tied and lowers her head to have her ears trimmed.

"Lil grows a coat like a buffalo."

"I've got some news. Dolgin gonna sponsor the race," she speaks up over the clippers.

He puts them in a can of kerosene to cool.

"The whole thing?"

"And ten thousand for the winner."

"The Toad's not so bad after all."

"You never know what he's up to."

"But he offered to pay for the whole shooting match."

"And we might be the target, we've got to protect ourselves."

"Surround the Hall with cannons, mine the canals." The mare kicks over the can and spills the kerosene. Clayton picks up the clippers, "It's a generous offer."

"Then you'll tell Ramser?"

"I wouldn't go that far. Maybe you could mention it on Sunday. GoGo's invited us all to watch the finals."

PALM BEACH POLO

Yellow Cartier banners flutter in the breeze. Bentleys and Jaguars stand fended to fender with shiny Chevy trucks and the Sanitation Marching Band is blasting Stars and Stripes Forever. Mendoza's box is front and center. GoGo, Ramser, Victoria, Clayton, and Alice are turned out in their Sunday chic. On the field, the Orange Mitsubishi Rice Rockets are playing fast and furious with Mendoza's Mimosas in blue.

Merlos Scores and the Crowd Cheers

Alice observes, "We could use this crowd at the steeplechase."

"What on earth for?" Ramser retorts.

"Remember? We've got land to sell and Banker Coldwell is about to foreclose while you run off the buyers."

"I get your drift. Suppose we wanted spectators. How would we get them?"

"Advertise and offer prize money."

"That is costly."

"Hard cash lures the fast horses. The media will be all over it."

"Where's the money coming from?"

A mini-skirted waitress brings another round of drinks. The Mimosas score another goal and Alice takes a long swallow.

"Dolgin will sponsor the race and there'll be $10,000 to the winner."

Ramser's reply reverberates, "No! The Everglades Cup has been run for decades without that double-dealing developer's dirty dollars."

GoGo turns around and gives him an angelic smile, "It sounds terrific. Can polo ponies race too?"

Alice is relieved. "Why not?"

"Good, I'll enter Rio. He's really fast."

GoGo's enthusiasm swivels Ramser from a brick to a sponge.

On the field, Merlos is driving his pony downfield galloping along under the flying ball. He raises his mallet and with a giant swing, reverses the flight, he spins his pony around, and drives home the winning goal. The fans stand and cheer.

MENDOZA'S VILLA

The victory party is well underway. The players and their camp followers are dancing around the pool. Victoria and Merlos are buttressing the bar and GoGo is gallivanting with the Mitsubishi Captain.

The blaring Disco Alfresco inspires Clayton and Alice to retreat inside the Villa. The walls are covered with high goal photos and shelves of silver trophies. "This looks like a shrine to equestrian field hockey …," her voice trails off, sensing they're not alone.

An upmarket English couple have also escaped the revelry. Gazing at a gilded bucket of polo balls, the gentleman remarks, "Quite something, these colonials."

"How do you do? I'm Clayton Hoopes and this is my friend Alice Liddell."

"Lord David and Lady Sybil Lloyd. We're foxhunters from Leicestershire. Isn't it all fantastic and aren't we lucky to be here?"

Clayton perks up. "We hunt The Palm Beach hounds."

Lord Lloyd raises an eyebrow, "Hunting this far south? It must get awfully warm."

"It does, but we start early and quit before noon."

"Sounds delightful. We must see your pack. We're staying at the Club on Hurlingham." Lady Lloyd smiles and ushers her husband out.

Back at the pool, the breeze has picked up, the music is winding down and the celebrants are taking their leave.

Victoria is over the top, "Merlos and I are flying down to Argentina tomorrow. Doesn't give you much notice, but we'd like you both to come along."

"No, er… I can't," Clayton answers defensively.

Merlos nods to Serena, "We spoke about your hunt country and the land you have for sale."

"Yes?"

"Perhaps we can put something together."

"It's awfully short notice."

Victoria chimes in, "Not to worry, we'll be back on Wednesday. You can meet us at General Aviation in Miami and pick up the money."

As they drive out the west gate, Alice asks, "What's wrong?"

"I don't like it, Mendoza is some kind of a crook. He can bring that money here himself. Besides, I have a meeting with the IRS."

"Well, at least we've got the steeple-chase sponsored."

Clayton laughs, "Did you see the look on Ramser's face when you told him Dolgin was backing it? Lucky GoGo was there. You can ride Clyde."

"Do you think it's safe?"

"Sure, he's won the race before. Just hang on and kick on — you can't kill Horatio's old horse."

"Thanks."

LORD AND LADY LLOYD

T he next day Alice is meeting the Lloyds at the Hall. Clayton is arranging invoices in chronological stacks. "Can't get up or I'll lose my place."

"Stay where you are."

Napoleon and Caesar race through the room sending the papers flying.

"I give up. The auditor can sort this out himself." Clayton throws the paperwork back in the muck basket.

Alice hears a car on the gravel drive, "That will be the Lloyds. Victoria gave me the scoop. David's an insurance tycoon—at Lloyds of London."

Napoleon and Caesar are wrestling on the lawn. Lady Sybil squints up at the Hall's lofty towers. "A little more of Disney World."

Alice serves a well-provisioned tea tray and toast rack. The Lord spreads his slice thick with butter and marmalade, and commences eating, "We've got a small castle in Sussex, a shooting box in Warwickshire, and this would be the perfect place to pop off for a bit of sun. January here is like July in Brighton."

Lady Lloyd adds, "This is the first wintertime I've ever been warm. I won't leave without taking a proper look around."

"We do have some land for sale," Alice ventures.

"What are the taxes like?" The Lord is devouring his third slice of toast.

Clayton stares in his cup, escaping among the tea leaves.

Alice is up to speed. "Florida has low property taxes, and no state income tax."

"The British Isles are eating us alive. We don't want to become tax exiles, but what choice do we have?"

Sybil adds, "The hunting after Christmas is ever so cold. What about the anti-blood sport people?"

Clayton's happy to get beyond the taxes, "The protests haven't caught on over here. What with our Constitution and the right to arm bears."

"Could we possibly see your pack?"

At the kennels, Bruno is dipping the hounds in a Sulphur bath under Ramser's watchful eye. The Bandersnatch turns around with a hound in hand and splashes Clayton with the odorous solution, "Best thing for mange or ringworm."

Alice introduces the Lloyds.

Ramser is pleased to meet the right sort, "Let's have the pack brought out."

The Huntsman brings out thirty-six hounds keeping them together with a pocketful of biscuits. "English purebreds like yourselves."

The guests inspect each hound from nose to stern. "Sybil is considering wintering in this part of the world."

Ramser is onboard, "Good, we must work together to fend off creeping commercialism."

Clayton doesn't want to go there. "We're having a steeplechase soon. Would you have an entry?"

"Indeed! We've been campaigning our horse Somerset in the Shires. We'll have him flown over, he'll love it here." Lady Lloyd is dreadfully sporting, "And we should survey the land and contact our solicitors."

"Well, there's polo at one, we must be going." David takes Sybil's arm as they depart.

"The Lady makes quick decisions." Alice is happy to note, "I bet she keeps the money on her side of the mattress."

Clayton looks at Alice's watch and startles, "Money, right, the IRS, I'm late."

ETERNAL REVENUE SERVICE

"Good Morning, Mr. Hoopes."

"Sorry I'm late…"

"What's that odor?" The auditor sniffs the air. "Smells like rotten eggs."

"The hounds were being dipped. Afraid I got too close, but Sulphur is good for mange and ringworm."

"And this?" Leffert Lefferts is not pleased with the muck basket on his desk.

"Oh, they're the records you asked for. I think they cover the last twenty years."

"The old paper dumping ploy. Trying to bury me under all this supposed documentation?"

"No, I..."

"Do you have an accountant or a lawyer?"

"A lawyer? Can I go to jail?"

"You can, if we can prove fraud— willfully hiding income, evading taxes, concealing property, perjury or falsifying records."

"Ambition, distraction, and multiplication, to the best of my knowledge, it is none of the above."

"For your sake, I hope not, but Horatio J. Hoopes, you better get yourself a lawyer."

"Horatio has gone to his final reward. I'm his son, Clayton."

Lefferts is crestfallen, "Damn, I finally corral a rampant tax dodger and he's dead. Well, you better take your records home and straighten them out. You'll be hearing from us."

"Would you like to go to lunch?" Clayton offers.

"The Government has a policy forbidding such things."

GENERAL AVIATION

Miami Dade General Aviation houses US Customs and Border Protection and offers services to private flights.

Alice arrives as the Dassault Falcon comes in sight. The plane lands on the asphalt runway.

Merlos and Victoria disembark. She is nervous. "The oil pressure went out on the flight back. The engines were seizing up. We were lucky to make it."

Merlos announces, "I'll watch the saddles go through customs."

"Then lunch at the Jockey Club?" Victoria is ready to move on.

"Whatever you say."

The enormous plane looks like a mountain crest with mechanics scaling the sides and dismantling the engines. A band of baggage handlers unloads the saddles and stacks them on six electric trailers.

"In Argentina this would take weeks," Merlos smiles.

At Customs, the saddles are precariously stacked next to the inspection table. Victoria moves to steady the pile.

"Please wait behind the blue line." The guard is right on it.

Merlos is filling out declarations in triplicate.

A German Shepard nudges Alice's knee.

"Just a routine inspection," announces the Agent.

The dog moves toward the saddles sniffing and growling. At a sign from his handler, Rollo attacks the pile. Saint George slaying the cowhide dragon, the dog grabs one from the bottom and a landslide begins. The top saddle is airborne on its own flight path and hits the ground with a crack. The cantle and underpinnings split open and a kilo of white crystals spills out on the terminal floor.

"Christ, I hope that's talcum powder," Alice exclaims.

Merlos watches the proceedings with a dispassionate eye and signals the ladies to leave while they still can. They make their way to Alice's green Toyota and drive off.

"No sense letting them collect more evidence." Victoria is still vibrating.

"Will they come after us?"

"I don't think so. We're the goldfish, they're after the sharks."

Victoria's phone rings. She listens attentively and frowns. "That was Mendoza's lawyer. He's going to need all that money for bail."

"What's Merlos going to do?"

"He's got plenty of irons in the fire."

"Well, they're starting to melt."

BACK AT BIG CYPRESS

Kicking Crawfish is still leaning against the refrigerator when Alice enters the trading post complaining, "It rained and poured, Loxahatchee canals overflowed and the roadbeds were washed out."

"Told you I was a rain dancer."

"I didn't ask for a deluge."

"You brought Camels not Kools - no refreshing taste of menthol. The cheap rum gave me a headache and the TV won't play my 'Little Big Man' DVD."

"You're nitpicking. I paid you to lift a curse, not for thunderstorms."

"I took my sick Grandmother to a hospital in Fort Lauderdale. She stayed two weeks and died. I'm still paying the bills. The doctor said, you don't always get what you pay for, but you always pay for what you get."

Alice has gambled and lost. "I need help."

White Eagle comes in and signals Crawfish to leave. The Medicine Man looks at Alice with inquiring eyes.

"I'm trying to…"

"Crawfish told me your story."

"He wanted cigarettes and talked about the Hopi prophecy predicting television…"

"The Hopis foretold many animals would die and man would cause rampant destruction. The Great Spirit says we must abolish evil and plant the seeds of peace. This is the work of the warrior today."

"I'm running out of time."

"Saturiba's spirit seeks retribution. While his ghost is abroad, no peace will dwell with his enemies."

"Can you lift the curse?"

The Medicine Man gestures towards the setting sun, "Tonight at the sacred fire, a Shaking Tent ceremony may appease the spirits."

The crickets chirp ceaselessly. A crescent moon lights the trail and a red owl calls to his mate. Alice follows three braves and the Medicine Man deep into the Everglades.

At the ceremonial grounds, a bonfire reflects in the Thunderbird's golden eyes. Below is the water panther, a powerful underworld creature, and finally a great horned serpent with a blazing ruby crest. In the flickering fire light, the braves set to work staking pine saplings in the ground and covering them with otter pelts.

White Eagle sheds his deerskins and clad only in a loincloth, enters the tepee to invoke the spirits in an ancient tongue. The incantation grows louder as he works himself into a frenzy. The tent begins to shake and the poles bend almost to the ground. The hooting owl gives way to a lone wolf's anguished cry. White Eagle performs the Ghost Dance and reunites with Saturiba's spirit. When he emerges from the tent the howling ceases.

"Saturiba's tomahawk must be returned. Without it, the Chief cannot enter the Happy Hunting Ground where no white man can go."

Alice remembers "Horatio used it to kill the fox, but where is it now?"

"The axe lets the winds of evil blow in under the roof. Return it to the grave and the curse will be lifted."

"When I retrieve the tomahawk, how do I find the grave?"

"Where did Horatio die?"

"The accident happened at a jump near the orange grove."

"It was no accident. Saturiba's spirit reached out from the grave."

THE HALL

Clayton is burning the midnight oil, sorting through his chaotic accounts.

Alice rushes in. "Come on, we've got to find the tomahawk."

"What?"

"White Eagle said we must put it back in the grave. Where is it?"

He goes on sorting out the statements.

"Come on now, think."

Clayton furrows his brow. "I used to play with a magic hatchet."

"Where?"

"In the attic"

They charge up the staircase.

The Cigar Store Indian's eyes follow Alice around the room, and the hobby horse mysteriously rocks back and forth.

"That horse looks real."

"He is. When Dobbin died, the Master had him stuffed and turned him out up here."

They search relentlessly through an old Calvary fortress and the overflowing toy chests.

"It must be here somewhere."

Outside, storm clouds send a cold wind through the attic. Alice starts to close a cobwebbed window with the shutters banging against the brick wall. As she reaches for the latch, her eyes fall on the axe wedged in place to keep them open.

"Clayton, look."

He bounds over to the window, and forces back the panels while she removes the weathered tomahawk and cradles it in her hands.

"Now I remember. I put it there to climb out on the roof and look at the stars."

There's a clap of thunder and the lights go out. Saturiba's spirit lurks in the attic.

"Time to bury the hatchet." Clayton throws a spade in the station wagon and they head out for the grove.

Alice walks in circles using the axe as a divining rod. The handle turns slowly and points to a spot near the jump.

Clayton's heel sinks in the shifting earth, "That's where Clyde slipped on takeoff." He begins digging furiously. The ground gives way as he breaks through the side of an earthen coffin.

Dark clouds eclipse the moon. The wind picks up and a yellowing skeletal hand reaches up for the tomahawk.

Alice stifles a scream. Clayton inters the axe and quickly covers the grave.

A shooting star brightens the night sky.

CALCUTTA

The sound of a helicopter reverberates overhead. Mort Waldorf has taken to county skies, this time displaying a banner, "Come one, and all to the Players Club for a Steeplechase Celebration and Calcutta Auction." Friday evening the gala is in full swing.

The Walrus And The Carpenter Adorn
Ritzy Crackers With Oysters.

As a teenager, Dolgin ran bets for
bookies in the South Bronx, he steps to
the podium and surveys the crowd. "It is
time to place your wagers. Rio is first up, a
sleek polo pony owned and ridden by
GoGo Mendoza. Who'll begin the
Beguine betting on this whirlwind entry?"

The polo crowd is right at home with GoGo.

"One thousand, two thousand, do I hear three?" Dolgin's delighted, Rio's prospects sell for seven thousand dollars.

Next on the list, the Wickstrom horses bring in eight hundred apiece.

Off in a corner, Ramser accosts Clayton. "I still don't like it."

Clayton has one ear on the bidding. "We've never had a crowd like this."

"I've checked on Dolgin and his pal Waldorf. They build retirement communities complete with nursing homes and funeral parlors. They're gonna destroy the hunt country."

The Hatter has gotten into the Champagne. "Let's enjoy life while we can."

Dolgin drones on. "Here we have Malibu, just flown in from his victory in the

Delmonte Gold Cup at Pebble Beach. He is owned and will be ridden by Victoria Valentine."

Victoria and Mort are marinated in several bottles of Cristal Brut. Mort never misses a swig, "Twenty-thousand." He buys her entry outright much to Victoria's delight and Dolgin's amazement.

Loxahatchee Lil and Collector's Item canter through the Calcutta, then Somerset and Gryphon are snapped up by the enthusiastic crowd.

The Toad is elated, "And last but not least, my own special entry, McGovern the mule, a fleet descendant of Arkansas' finest."

A well-endowed Gilded Age matron bats her eyes at the Master of Ceremonies, "One thousand dollars."

"Two thousand do I hear two?"

The matron bids "two."

Sold to the highest bidder.

Alice thinks to herself, *an auction. What a good idea*, and she hatches a plan.

CAUCUS RACE

T he rising sun squints balefully through the orange blossoms as a dozen horses warm up over the practice pickets erected on the Lion Country Safari lawn. On the side-lines, trainers, grooms, and well-heeled punters survey the entries. In the midst of the action, Alice is mounted on Clyde hoping to learn the nuances of racing over fences.

Clayton trots over on Loxahatchee Lil, "Let's give it a go."

They gallop head to head halfway around the field and approach a good-size post and rail. Clyde gathers momentum and carries Alice over the first jump, then lowers his head down and charges the next fence completely out of control. It's two and a half times around before she can stop.

"I can't hold one side of him."

"Just point him toward home and hang on. The finish line is back at his barn and the sooner he gets there the better."

Victoria is wearing a British racing green sweater with a large blue cross emblazoned on the front.

She canters over on Malibu, her racy Appaloosa.

"I like you outfit," Clayton offers.

"The blue cross is for the he emergency room. Reminds them I'm insured."

Ramser is trotting around the field on Collector's Item. Horse and rider are both long in the tooth. Bruno Mangus, in a bright red t-shirt is riding Gryphon in the Master's wake. The Huntsman has strict

instructions to block and tackle the com-
petition.

The Dynamic Duo bear a Striking
Resemblance to Don Quixote and
Sancho Panza.

Somerset, the Lloyd's English racer, walks down the wide ramp of a huge commercial carrier. David gives his jockey a leg up while the horse stares at the Lion Country landscape and tries to get oriented through glazed eyes.

GoGo is galloping flat out up and down the field but she can't get Rio near the jumps.

A large U-Haul truck pulls in. Dolgin's gopher—ex-jockey, Buzzy Hanscome is at the wheel. The boss follows close behind in his vintage Mercedes which has be repaired and repainted in the Land's End colors, fire engine red with yellow racing stripes.

"Hee-haw, Hee-haw" Buzzy lowers the ramp, and Mc Govern leaps out to greet the crowd.

"What the Hell is that?" Ramser's inquiring mind wants to know.

"What's it look like?" Dolgin retorts.

"Why, you can't run a mule in the Everglades Derby."

"Who says so? I'm putting up the stakes and I'll make the rules."

"Over my dead body."

"Don't be hasty, Prince. Save it for the race."

Alice rides over. "What's with the mule?"

"If the Master can run that has-been heirloom, you can't fault a young healthy hybrid."

A bull elephant's thunderous trumpeting interrupts the conversation. Everyone turns to see the herd of Hortons spectating from the far side of a cyclone fence. Clyde leaps forward ready to run.

Clayton reaches out to steady the horse, "That's a good sign. If he's raring to go at the start, then he should be first at the finish."

Alice takes a short hold of her reins, "I hope we get to the starting line."

Victoria's horse is impervious to the pachyderms.

Alice is envious. "All this noise doesn't bother him?"

"I stuff wool plugs in his ears."

Lord Lloyd is escorting his distracted horse to the paddock, "It's a zoo! They're racing through a bloody zoo."

A young girl in a Land's End visor hands Lady Lloyd a four-colored glossy brochure replete with a projected panorama of the Wonderland Country Club and a golf course.

Sybil mutters to herself, "Why on earth would they put a golf course in the middle of hunt country? Terribly American."

An old green Land Rover drives by. Hildreth is camouflaged by a pith helmet and aviator sunglasses.

The horses are at the post. Mort raises his shotgun, fires both barrels in the air, and they're off. Several stray pellets land on McGovern, the mule lets out a furious bawl and leaps into the lead for twenty strides until Rio surges ahead.

Alice tucks Clyde in behind the mule and one mile out they gallop past a 'road closed' sign. Buzzy takes a left and jumps McGovern over the saw-horse blockade, Ramser and Bruno follow the detour.

GoGo and Rio are going wide, racing straight along the edge of Southern Boulevard, avoiding the major obstacles but adding some distance to the course.

Alice cringes at a massive billboard emblazoned with "The Site of Your Future Home" posted among the palm trees.

A littler further along, a pile of decapitated palmettos forms an imposing wall. "Ride for a Piece of the Promised Land" adorns the fence in neon lights.

"The Terrible Toad strikes again," shouts Ramser, as he charges the jump with rhino ferocity.

Bruno slows Gryphon down, allowing the Wickstroms to come along side, and they all jump together. Once in the air the Huntsman pulls on his right rein, getting his horse sideways and crashing into Iona who falls and knocks Dick off. The spectators applaud the Demolition Derby while the angry couple yell "foul" and follow their horses back toward the elephants.

The Huntsman survives the carnage and gallops toward the water hazard intent on sabotaging McGovern who is trotting through the pond. The Bandersnatch pulls the mule's bridle half off and pushes his head under water. McGovern resurfaces with ears flat back and teeth bared. He grabs his adversary's arm, chomps down mercilessly and drags him under. When the mule finally lets go, Bruno floats to the surface and backstrokes to the bank, unable to go on.

Unfortunately, in the fracas, Buzz's batteries and the electric wires short circuit and his hot spurs backfire. The shocked mule plunges out of the water. Buzz is magnetized to the hot-wired hybrid who charges into the underbrush at a dead run.

Another Land's End sign looms ahead in a clump of palmettos, "A Low Down Payment Will Put You in the Sporting Set." Next up, sixteen cypress trunks are piled in an awesome pyramid. The electrified mule stands back and leaps but his best efforts only land him on the topmost logs, where he is suspended and unable to regain his footing.

Alice is following six lengths behind and sees the calamity—too late. She closes her eyes and takes a death grip on the reins. Clyde never slackens his pace. In a prodigious leap, he clears the logs and the floundering mule and gallops on to the spectators' applause.

Somerset, with his English jockey, is coming up fast. Alice looks around for a moment and then back to the trail just as a steam shovel with a front loader is driven directly across her path. The operator throws a lever forward and the earth mover's giant claw rises up and reaches for them. She flails at the reins to keep Clyde out of range, but Horatio's horse is heading for home and well beyond the turning point. She shuts her eyes and hears his horseshoes click over the case-hardened steel as they clear the obstacle racing onward.

Somerset and his rider are not so lucky. The Lloyd's entry stops on a dime and hurls his English jockey into the bucket.

The crowd cheers as Clyde charges first over the finish line. Alice hardly realizes the race is over and she's won. Clayton, Victoria, and GoGo finish in that order and Ramser is a distant fifth.

TO THE WINNER

Dolgin's mounts the stage in front of Everglades Hall. The sound systems squeals and all eyes turn in his direction. "Ladies and Gentlemen your attention please. Don't miss this opportunity to reserve your very own site in the Hunting Homelands. Let me remind you that our sale's booths are open with agents at the ready."

"And without further ado, The Land's End Corporation would like to present Alice Liddell with the winner's check for $10,000 and this beautiful trophy." Dolgin holds a silver-plated bulldozer and the check aloft while the Junior College marching band strikes up the Camptown Races. "Great performance," Dolgin presents the trophy. She juggles it for a moment and hands it back.

"I would like to thank Jordan Dolgin and Land's End for sponsoring the race." Alice opens with her own Queen's Gambit, "And I have a special announcement. Right here and now three thousand acres of prime Hoopes property will be sold at auction. This is a golden opportunity to buy land direct from the seller with no intermediaries."

"You can't do that!" Dolgin declines the gambit loses his cool and drops the bulldozer on his foot.

Alice moves on, "Bruno Mangus of Cattle Auction fame will conduct the bidding."

Somewhere in the crowd, Banker Coldwell calls out "I protest."

The crowd is buzzing. No one takes any notice of the objections. Alice adjusts the amplifiers and hands Bruno the microphone.

"Welcome to the Hunt Country Auction."

"Welcome yourself, you can't use this platform." Dolgin won't quit without a fight.

"It's on my land," Clayton rises to the occasion and then to Bruno. "Just go ahead and sell those acres, we don't hunt out there anyway."

"Ladies and gentlemen, let's start the bidding. Who'll give a thousand for the first acre?"

"He used to start the bulls higher than that," Ramser points out.

Half the audience raise their hands. They're in.

"Two thousand, I have three thousand, do I see four… In the back there's eight." The bids are coming in fast and furious, at thirty-seven thousand the action slows down.

Iona Wickstrom is waving both hands in the air, "Thirty-eight thousand, we bid thirty-eight thousand, do you hear that Dick?"

Dick Wickstrom stands by shaking his head.

Dolgin is puffing hard on a Cohiba Esplendido, Coldwell is grinding his teeth and standing at parade rest.

Another bidder goes for thirty-nine.

Bruno asks for forty.

Iona shrieks "Forty-thousand."

"Sold to the Wickstroms" The auctioneer bangs down his gavel and Alice records the purchase.

Bruno starts the next lot at forty-thousand and six voices raise it to forty-one. Coldwell watches intently.

Dolgin raises a bullhorn so as not to be overlooked, "Forty-two thousand."

"Forty-five," Coldwell joins the action.

The public backs off when the big guns come in.

"Forty-eight, I'll pay that for every last acre," Dolgin takes a stand.

Bruno whoops! The bidders are in full cry.

"That's it for me, let them have the Damn Swamp." The Banker loses his temper and the land.

Alice turns to Clayton, "Poor Rumple Coldwell, spinning the Master's straw into gold for twenty years."

"Forty-eight once, forty-eight twice," Bruno bangs the gavel.

Another bid from the back, "Fifty-thousand for each and every acre."

"Any more bids?" Bruno waves his gavel high, preserving the extravagant moment, "going, going, gone! Sold to Mr. Waldorf, two thousand nine hundred and ninety-nine acres at fifty-thousand each."

The Red King and Queen, are Grinning
like Cheshire Cats.

The reporters are pressing Clayton for his reaction.

Bruno asks, "Can we get some more hounds, now that we can feed them?"

Victoria commandeers the media, "Wonderland will have it all, six champion-ship polo fields, stables for four hundred horses, golf courses, a tennis complex and a spa."

Mort has surrendered his heart and his wallet "Don't forget the shopping mall and the racetrack."

"I just ran out of breath."

A little black Dachshund runs over and nips at Alice's heels. She follows Serendipity, Hildreth is sitting in the gazebo smiling for the first time. The curse is lifted and her silver albatross has been replaced with a golden horseshoe. "Thanks to you, the storm is over and I can stop battening down the hatches."

"I know Clayton will want to see you. He's probably down at the stable."

"I remember, he always tells the horses, what happens, good or bad."

As they enter the barn, Clayton tossing a generous flake of alfalfa to each horse.

"You missed one, sonny."

"No, I…"

He turns, catches his mother's eye, drops the hay, and rushes to her side. They embrace and twenty years of painful separation melt away in a timeless moment.

"I saw you bouncing along in the Land Rover. I knew you'd come back."

"Never replace those old sand roads. I tried to pave over my feelings. It doesn't work. I longed to see you, but the time was never right."

Clyde whinnies for his alfalfa.

"Mr. Waldorf is giving you a fortune for the land. You might set up a trust for the Loxahatchee Wildlife Refuge. That'll keep the alligators and the taxman happy."

Clayton is relieved at the suggestion. "You're probably right, but what are you going to do?"

"Sail away. I'd be landlocked here. Besides, nobody wants their mother running the show. You kids will be fine." She embraces her son for a moment, gives Alice a hug and quietly leaves.

Clyde paws at the stall door till Clayton brings his alfalfa.

ALL'S WELL THAT ENDS WELL

Tonight, the attic shutters are open to the sparkling stars. The White Rabbit blows "gone away" on his horn while Dobbin gallops Through the Looking Glass with Alice and the Hatter onboard.

www.ingramcontent.com/pod-product-compliance
Lightning Source LLC
Chambersburg PA
CBHW060551260626
47161CB00003B/1154